D0467609

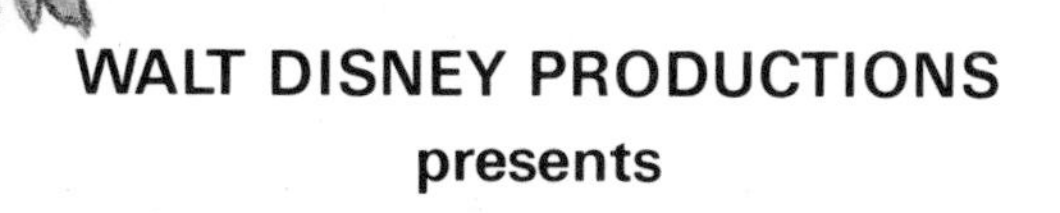

WALT DISNEY PRODUCTIONS
presents

Li'l Wolf and the Three Wishes

Random House New York

Book Club Edition

 Published in the United States by Random House, Inc., New York, and simultaneously in Canada by Random House of Canada Limited, Toronto. Originally published in Denmark as LILLE ULV OG DE TRE ØNSKER by Gutenberghus Gruppen, Copenhagen. ISBN: 0-394-87119-7 Manufactured in the United States of America
4567890 ABCDEFGHIJK

One day Li'l Wolf went for a walk with his friends the three little pigs.

"Let's go deep into the woods! Follow me!" said Li'l Wolf.

Finally Li'l Wolf stopped walking.
"I think we've gone far enough,"
Li'l Wolf said. "Let's turn back now.
Who knows what we might meet here?"

"You're right,"
said Practical Pig.
"I would not want
to meet your father,
the Big Bad Wolf,
here in the woods!"

Suddenly a cry rang out—"HELP!"

"Go see what that is, Li'l Wolf," said Practical Pig. "We'll wait here. Maybe your father is playing a trick."

Li'l Wolf followed the cry for help.
He looked around carefully.
But there was no one to be seen.

Then the voice called out again.
"Over here! And hurry! Ow! It hurts!"

Li'l Wolf looked at the nearest tree.
It was talking!
"I can't believe it!" Li'l Wolf said.
"Gee, am I seeing things?"

"No, but I'm feeling things! Ouch!" said the tree. "Someone nailed this sign onto me. Will you please remove it?"

"I'll be glad to," said Li'l Wolf.
He tugged hard at the sign.
Cree-aak! The sign came off!
"Ahh!" sighed the tree happily.
"That's much better!"

"I want to thank you. Please pick one of my magic plums," said the tree. "But be careful—it grants three wishes!"

"Thanks!" said Li'l Wolf, and he picked a plum from the tree.

Li'l Wolf hurried back to the pigs. They were hiding behind a rock.

"You can come out. It's safe now," Li'l Wolf said.

"Who was calling for help?"
the pigs asked.

"It was a tree," Li'l Wolf said.
"It had a sign nailed onto its side.
The sign was hurting the tree."

"You're making fun of us, Li'l Wolf!"
said Practical Pig. "Trees can't talk!"

“This tree did talk!” said Li’l Wolf. “And it gave me a magic plum. See? The plum will give me three wishes.”

“Ho, ho!” laughed Practical Pig. “You’ve read too many fairy tales!”

Li’l Wolf was mad.

He did not say anything more about the magic plum.

It was almost time for dinner.

Li'l Wolf and the three pigs set off for home.

Li'l Wolf came
to the path that
led to his house.

He waved good-bye
to his friends.

"I'll show this magic plum to my dad. He'll believe me!" Li'l Wolf said.

But the Big Bad Wolf was not in the house.
Li'l Wolf saw a note on the table.
The note was from the Big Bad Wolf.

LI'L WOLF -
GO CHOP SOME
FIREWOOD.
I'LL BE BACK SOON,
DAD

Li'l Wolf put his magic plum on the table.

He went outside to chop firewood.

"It's strange how Dad always comes home AFTER the wood is all chopped," Li'l Wolf said.

The Big Bad Wolf hid behind a tree.
"Ha, ha! Li'l Wolf is almost finished chopping the wood. Now I can go home!" the Big Bad Wolf said.
And off he went.

The Big Bad Wolf saw the plum at once.
"Yum—a plum!" said the Big Bad Wolf.
He took a big bite out of the plum.
"What an awful taste!" said the wolf.
And he threw the plum in the garbage.

Li’l Wolf walked in just then.

“Oh, no, Dad! The plum—did you eat the plum that was here?” Li’l Wolf asked.

“What’s the fuss about? That plum tasted awful!” said the Big Bad Wolf.

“But it was a magic plum. Now it won’t work,” said Li’l Wolf.

“A magic plum? What nonsense! Stop being silly—and start making dinner,” snorted the Big Bad Wolf.

Li'l Wolf began to cry.
"I don't feel well," Li'l Wolf said.
"I wish you would make dinner, Dad."

WHOOSH! The Big Bad Wolf was pulled toward the kitchen shelves.

"What's going on?" cried the wolf.

The Big Bad Wolf opened cans of beans.

He did not mean to—but he could not stop!

The Big Bad Wolf lit the stove.
He threw the beans in a pot.

The Big Bad Wolf stirred the beans. He blinked his eyes in surprise.

"What's making me cook the dinner like this?" the Big Bad Wolf said.

"Even though you ate the magic plum, it still works– it granted me a wish! And I have two left!" Li'l Wolf said.

"Is that so?" asked the Big Bad Wolf.

"Yes! I wished you would fix dinner—and you did," Li'l Wolf said.

"Well, I'll make the next wish," said the Big Bad Wolf. "Heh, heh!"

The Big Bad Wolf
took the magic plum
out of the garbage.

"You see, I only
took one bite,"
the Big Bad Wolf said
to Li'l Wolf.

Li'l Wolf was happy that his dad
thought the plum was magic.

But Li'l Wolf did not know
what his dad was up to!

"Go ahead and wish," Li'l Wolf said.
The Big Bad Wolf licked his lips.
"I wish the three little pigs were
here. Ho, ho!" said the Big Bad Wolf.
"Oh, no!" cried Li'l Wolf.

WHOOSH! The three pigs were blown from their home straight to the house of the Big Bad Wolf!

"Help!" the pigs cried. "Help! We can't stop!"

“Hello there, porkchops! How nice of you to drop in!” said the Big Bad Wolf.

“Oh, dear! The wishing plum worked again!” Li’l Wolf said.

“I believe in that magic plum now!” said Practical Pig. “But it’s too late!”

“I’ll make dinner now—and you pigs are invited!” said the Big Bad Wolf.

"Just a minute, Dad!" said Li'l Wolf. "There's still one more wish left—and I'm going to use it!"

The pigs looked at their friend. Could Li'l Wolf save them?

The Big Bad Wolf
scowled at his son.

"All right," the Big Bad Wolf said. "But don't you dare wish these pigs out of my arms, Li'l Wolf!"

Li'l Wolf knew he had to obey his dad.
"Don't worry," Li'l Wolf said. "I have a better idea.... I wish that you and the three pigs could be good friends!"

WHOOSH! The Big Bad Wolf found himself dancing with the little pigs!

The three pigs squealed with delight.

"Hurray for magic wishing plums!" said Li'l Wolf.

He joined the dancing friends.

"I can't believe I'm playing with pigs!" the Big Bad Wolf said. "How awful!"

"Don't feel bad," Li'l Wolf said to his dad. "The magic will probably go away in a few days. Then you'll be your old self again!"

“That was a good third wish,” said Practical Pig to Li’l Wolf. “From now on I will always believe in magic plums with wishes!”